THE SPIDERWICK CHRONICLES

MAKE-YOUR-OWN
FIELD GUIDE

D1283341

By Benjamin Harper
Based on the screenplay by
Karey Kirkpatrick and David Berenbaum and John Sayles
From the books by
Tony DiTerlizzi and Holly Black

An imprint of Simon & Schuster Children's Publishing Division
New York   London   Toronto   Sydney
1230 Avenue of the Americas, New York, NY 10020

Book manufactured in the United States of America
Crayons manufactured in China
First Edition
2 4 6 8 10 9 7 5 3 1
ISBN-13: 978-1-4169-5091-2
ISBN-10: 1-4169-5091-5

PARAMOUNT PICTURES AND NICKELODEON MOVIES PRESENT A KENNEDY/MARSHALL AND A MARK CANTON PRODUCTION A MARK WATERS FILM "THE SPIDERWICK CHRONICLES" FREDDIE HIGHMORE MARY-LOUISE PARKER NICK NOLTE WITH JOAN PLOWRIGHT AND DAVID STRATHAIRN VOICES BY SETH ROGEN MARTIN SHORT SPECIAL VISUAL EFFECTS BY INDUSTRIAL LIGHT & MAGIC VISUAL EFFECTS BY TIPPETT STUDIO MUSIC BY JAMES HORNER COSTUME DESIGNER JOANNA JOHNSTON EDITED BY MICHAEL KAHN A.C.E. PRODUCTION DESIGNER JAMES BISSELL DIRECTOR OF PHOTOGRAPHY CALEB DESCHANEL, ASC EXECUTIVE PRODUCERS JULIA PISTOR TONY DiTERLIZZI HOLLY BLACK PRODUCED BY MARK CANTON LARRY FRANCO ELLEN GOLDSMITH VEIN KAREY KIRKPATRICK BASED ON THE BOOKS BY TONY DiTERLIZZI AND HOLLY BLACK SCREENPLAY BY KAREY KIRKPATRICK AND DAVID BERENBAUM AND JOHN SAYLES DIRECTED BY MARK WATERS

SpiderwickChronicles.com

The Invisible World and its
inhabitants are all around
us—brownies, goblins, sprites,
and many other fantastic and
wonderful beings share the earth with
us. Some are friendly and some aren't.
You have the Sight—the ability to see
into the Invisible World and all of the
amazing creatures that most only think
of as fantasy!

Use this field guide to keep a record of
the mysterious creatures you discover in
your travels, but be careful—sometimes
they can be mischievous and even
dangerous! Take care to stay hidden and
not disturb them as you record your
observations.

PREPARE FOR YOUR EXPLORATION

Below are the essential things you'll need for tracking faeries.
Place a check next to each item to make sure you've got everything!

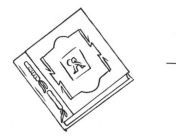

_____ *Your field guide!*

_____ *A magnifying glass
to study small creatures and look for clues.*

_____ *A bag of salt for protection
if you meet a nasty faerie—they don't like it!*

_____ *A flashlight for nighttime hunting.*

_____ *A backpack to carry everything.*

ARTHUR SPIDERWICK'S GUIDE TO THE FANTASTICAL WORLD

Uncle Arthur kept a very thorough guide of the creatures he studied. He documented their habits and included even the tiniest details of their appearance. *Use this page from his guide as a reference for how to study the Invisible World. Remember: Leave nothing out!*

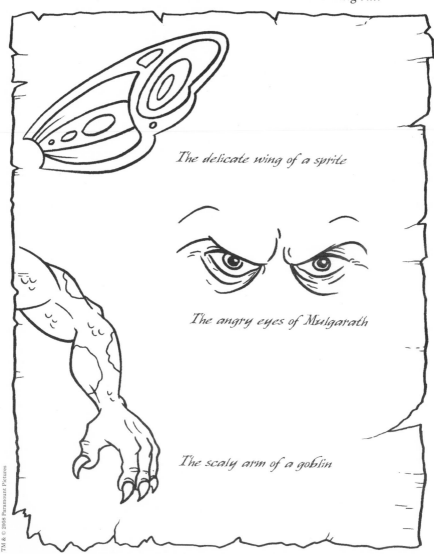

The delicate wing of a sprite

The angry eyes of Mulgarath

The scaly arm of a goblin

WELCOME, BROWNIE!

You've got a brownie in your house! Brownies are small, friendly creatures who like to keep things clean. Have you heard any skittering and scratching in the walls? Better yet—have you seen one?

Search every nook and cranny of your house until you find a brownie. Then, draw what it looks like here.

BROWNIE FACT SHEET

Monitor your brownie and keep a record of what you see. Then write down the things you've learned about it. (Don't forget to update it often!)

Name:

_____

Hobbies:

_____

_____

Clothing:

_____

_____

Location in home:

_____

_____

Clues that you had a brownie in your house:

_____

_____

Collections:

_____

_____

APARTMENT GUIDE

What does your brownie's habitat look like?
What did you find inside of it? *Draw it.*

BOGGART ALERT!

Have you lost anything that you can't find? Guess what . . . you've got a boggart! *Draw your boggart here and record its name!*

Name: _____

_____

Date: _____

IT'S A MEAN ONE!

Boggarts are mean brownies.
Can you tell which one is the boggart? *Circle it.*

LET'S BE FRIENDS

You can turn a boggart back into a friendly brownie by giving
it some honey to eat. Do you see any honey in this kitchen?
The brownie will make sure the boggart eats some, fast!
Draw a jar of honey in the brownie's hand.

GOBS OF GOBLINS

There are gobs of goblins hiding in this picture! How many can you find? *Read the checklist below and then circle each one you find in the picture. Then color them all green for future reference!*

_____ Short, stumpy, frog-like bodies

_____ White, pupil-less eyes

_____ Scaly skin

_____ Teeth made out of jagged glass and stone

WING IT!

You've found a sprite in your yard!
Sprites like to blend in with their surroundings.
Color in its beautiful wings, then color the flowers the same way.

BERRY BERRY GOOD!

Sprites love berries. Can you unscramble the names of these berries? *Complete each word on the lines, and then you can color in the sprites.*

C L A B K _____ berries

W R A T S _____ berries

L E B U _____ berries

R A N C _____ berries

GARDEN SURPRISE

**You were picking some flowers from your garden and
accidentally caught a sprite!** *Write about this in your journal.*

Date: _____

What kind of flowers were you picking? _____

What color were they? _____

What did you do with the sprite? _____

SAUCY SOLUTION

Tomato sauce keeps goblins away! Goblins will stay away when you eat it! Which of the snacks below is made with tomato sauce? *Circle it.*

ICE CREAM

CUPCAKES

PIZZA

POPCORN

POTATO CHIPS

Next, write in your journal about how the snack protected you.
Finish the story below:

Date: _____

It was time for lunch. I walked into the kitchen and

saw a goblin in the window! I know goblins don't like tomato

sauce, so I decided to eat some _____.

and the goblin _____

_____

_____

_____

_____

INVISIBLE WORLD JOURNAL PAGE

Write down what you've discovered so far!

POP QUIZ

**When studying the creatures of the Invisible World,
it is easy to become confused.** *Take this quick quiz to
make sure your senses are still sharp as a tack. Draw
a line from the creature's name to what it looks like.*

GOBLIN

BROWNIE

SPRITE

TINY WONDERS

Sprites are tiny! They are often mistaken for insects or flowers.
Practice sketching a sprite here.

PETAL PRETTY

Sprites like to use flowers for clothing.
Help this sprite look its best.

BERRY DELIGHT

After you've observed sprites, you'll surely have noticed the delicious-looking berries they eat. *Look closely, but don't eat them—you'll never want human food again. Draw the sprites' beautiful berries.*

INVISIBLE WORLD JOURNAL PAGE

Have you found anything unusual outside?
Write about it here!

Date: _____

_____

_____

_____

_____

_____

_____

_____

_____

_____

_____

CATCH OF THE DAY

Hogsqueal is a hobgoblin! Hobgoblins love to eat birds.
Hogsqueal just ate one bird but he's still hungry!
Draw another bird in the sky for Hogsqueal to try and catch.

WHO'S THERE?

What is happening in the water?
Write down a story below.

WATER WORLD

Draw the water creature you observed here.

WHO TOOK THE BOOK?

Thimbletack likes to speak in rhyme.
Can you finish this rhyme for him?

I tried to protect the book, you see,

I kept it under lock and key.

But Jared had to take a look . . .

_____

ALL IS CALM . . . NOT!

To someone who does not have the Sight, this looks
like a really peaceful house. *Color it in.*

THE REAL DEAL

Here's the house as viewed through the Seeing Stone. Not so peaceful now, is it? Thank goodness for the Protective Circle!

Take a good look so you'll remember it, and take notes!

Notes: _____

_____

THE A-MAZE-ING BOOK

Help Thimbletack get safely through this maze and to the book.
Watch out for goblins—and don't let Thimbletack stop to eat any honey!

START

FINISH

COLOR ME SCARY!

Have you had a nightmare that you're being chased?
Color this goblin green and give it a name.

Name: _____

_____

Date: _____

GETTING TO KNOW GOBLINS

Goblins can be very dangerous. Be careful while you observe them.
Write down the important things you've learned during your study.

Date: _____

Was the goblin traveling alone

or in a pack? _____

_____

Strange noises:

_____

Eating habits:

_____

_____

How did the goblin interact with its surroundings? Other goblins?

_____

_____

_____

_____

DINNERTIME!

Hobgoblins are friendly, unless you are a bird.
Then they are hungry! *Study this hobgoblin carefully.*

WHAT'S DIFFERENT?

You are developing a keen eye for the seen and unseen.
Now, test your strengths. *Without looking back at the previous page, describe how this hobgoblin is different from the other.*

Description: _____

_____

_____

OH, NO! A TROLL!

If you were unfortunate enough to come across a troll in your explorations, you've surely observed plenty about their horrible nature. *Record your findings below.*

Date: _____

Habitat: _____

Diet: _____

Description: _____

_____

_____

Alone or surrounded by goblins? _____

_____

Sleeping or awake? _____

Noises or speech: _____

OOH, AN OGRE!

Use this page to sketch an ogre.

SHAPE SHIFTING

Ogres can change into people or things to disguise themselves. They use this trait for evil. What did the ogre you observed change into? *Use this page to sketch the ogre's different images.*

FIRST LOOK

You've discovered a creature no one has ever seen before! *Draw what it looks like and give it a name. (Don't forget to sign and date your drawing!)*

Creature name: _____

Name: _____

Date: _____

AN INTRODUCTION

The Graces want to know all about your new creature.
Write down what you've discovered about it.

Date: _____

Suspected species: _____

Where found: _____

Eating habits: _____

_____

Habitat: _____

_____

_____

Interesting facts: _____

_____

_____

_____

Did you make contact? _____

_____

Answers

It's a Mean One!

Gobs of Goblins

Berry Berry Good!

CLABK _BLACK_ berries

WRATS _STRAW_ berries

LEBU _BLUE_ berries

RANC _CRAN_ berries

Saucy Solution

ICE CREAM

CUPCAKES

PIZZA

POPCORN

POTATO CHIPS

Answers

Pop Quiz

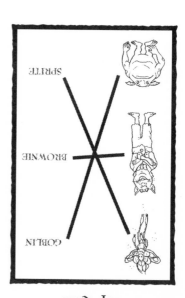

GOBLIN   BROWNIE   SPRITE

The A-maze-ing Book

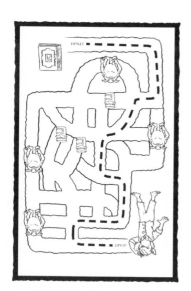

What's Different?

This goblin's clothes are ragged.

This goblin is wearing sandals.

This goblin has no bird.

This goblin is wearing a scarf.

LOOK FOR THESE OTHER GREAT
SPIDERWICK CHRONICLES
BOOKS FROM SIMON SCRIBBLES!

Uncle Arthur's Art Studio

Thimbletack's Activity Book

Hogsqueal's Activity Book

Spiderwick Stained Glass Book